For Freya
M.G.
For Liam
J.N.

First edition for the United States and Canada
published 1992 by Barron's Educational Series, Inc.

First published in 1992 by J.M. Dent & Sons Ltd,
91 Clapham High Street, London SW4 7TA.

Text copyright © 1992 Margaret Greaves.
Illustrations copyright © 1992 Jan Nesbitt.

All inquiries should be addressed to:
Barron's Educational Series, Inc.
250 Wireless Boulevard
Hauppauge, New York 11788

Library of Congress Catalog Card No. 92-2691

International Standard Book No. 0-8120-6294-9
International Standard Book No. 0-8120-9270-8
Library of Congress Cataloging-in-Publication Data

Greaves, Margaret.
     The star horse/by Margaret Greaves; illustra-
tions by Jan Nesbitt.
          p.   cm.
     Summary: An old carousel horse is granted
his wish and takes the boy who loves him on a
search to find the greatest horses of all.
     ISBN 0-8120-6294-9
     [1. Merry-go-round—Fiction.   2. Horses—
Fiction. 3. Wishes—Fiction.]   I. Nesbitt, Jan, ill.
II. Title.
PZ7.G8Ss 1992   92-2691
[E]—dc20   CIP
                                                            AC

PRINTED IN ITALY
2345   987654321

THE STAR HORSE

MARGARET GREAVES · JAN NESBITT

BARRON'S

Toby was old and tired. The other carousel horses were newer than he was. They laughed at his peeling paint and his chipped left ear. Sometimes Toby saw real horses and wished he were like them instead of being stiff and wooden and always going round and round and round.

"We must get rid of Toby," said the carousel owner one night. "He's so shabby that no one wants to ride him. I'm getting a new horse in his place."

Toby sighed. He'd expected this for a long time. Then he felt warm arms around his neck and hot tears on his nose. It was Paul, the carousel owner's son, who had always loved him. He would often sit on Toby when all the visitors had gone, just talking to him about this or that.

"You're the best carousel horse in the world," Paul told him. "I won't let them take you away. I *won't* ! I WON'T!"

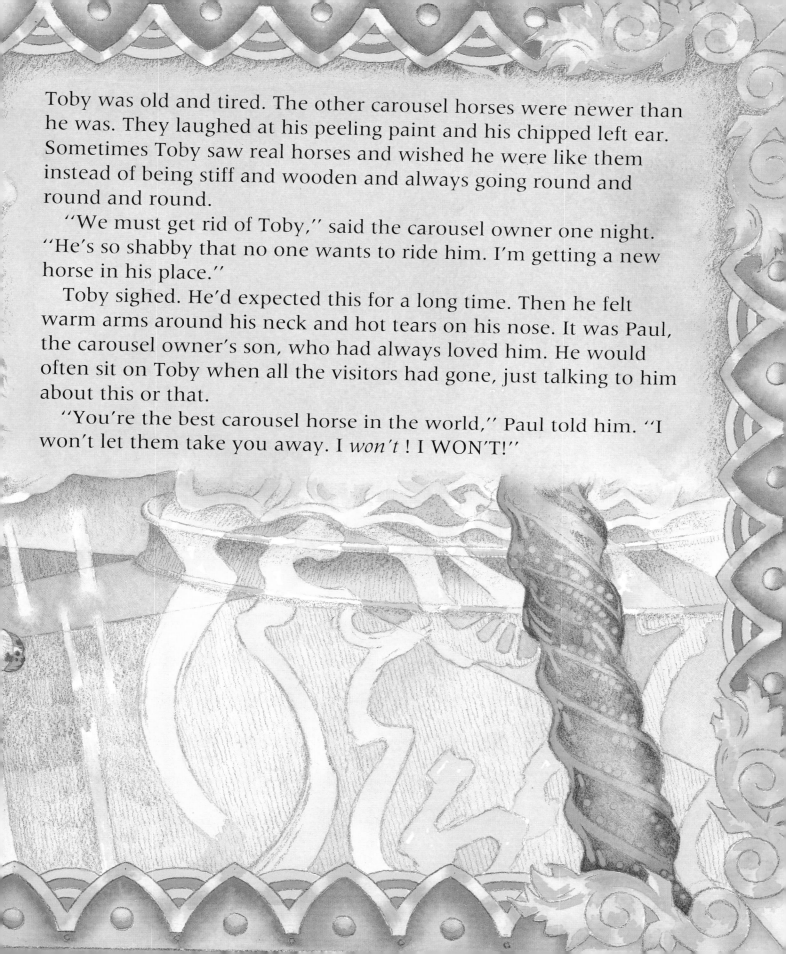

The old horse longed to comfort him, but his painted eyes could only stare unwinking at the streetlight over the road.

The light had never been so bright before. It grew and spread until it was as big as a stable door, and inside the light there was a shape like that of a young horse.

"Toby," it whinnied, "I am sent by the Great Horse Lord of the Sky to grant you a wish. Ask whatever you like."

Toby had all sorts of hopes, but there was something which was more important than any of them.

"Please," he said, "please, comfort my friend Paul when they send me away."

"He shall be comforted," said the messenger. "But you have asked a gift for him and not for you. What will you ask for yourself?"

"There is one thing," said Toby humbly. "I am old and plain, but I would love, just once, to see the greatest of all horses."

"Be free then, and seek him," said the shining creature.

The next minute Toby found himself, with Paul perched on his back, not on the carousel, but trotting like a real pony in a field beside the sea.

He kicked up his heels like a colt and whinnied for the sheer joy of it, while Paul laughed and held tight to his mane.

Then they saw the other horses, glossy in the pale light of the moon.

They were grazing on a bit of grassy land that ran out toward the sea. At Toby's whinny they raised their heads and neighed in response.

Timidly he approached them. He thought he had never seen creatures so beautiful.

"Surely," he said, "you must be the greatest of all horses!"

A bay stallion arched his splendid neck.

"We are the finest in all the land," he agreed.

They were pleased by Toby's admiration and let him graze with them, and were friendly and gentle with Paul.

Toward morning a strong breeze blew up, and white breakers rolled in on the flood tide.

"Look! Look! How fast they are coming! Gallop, before they can catch us," warned one of the herd.

The whole group wheeled and jostled nervously away, while Toby and Paul looked sadly after them.

Then they saw the line of white seahorses, foaming and frisking, striding the waves toward the shore. Their manes and tails streamed like silver banners.

"Surely," said Toby, "you must be the greatest of all horses, for the others are afraid of you."

The nearest creatures reared proudly, thrashing their forefeet so that water swirled around Toby's hooves.

"We are the finest horses in all the Seven Seas," they cried in voices that screamed like gulls.

Toby was too excited to be afraid. Paul climbed onto his back again and they raced along the edge of the tide, while the seahorses played beside them in the foam. Then the wind blew still more strongly.

"Faster! Faster!" called one of them. "The horses of the wind are driving behind us."

Line after line they thundered past, and behind them came the horses of the wind. Black as storm clouds, gray as rain, dappled with crimson or fleeced with white, they swept down over the sea. Toby bowed his head before their beauty.

"Surely," he said, "*you* are the greatest of all horses, for even the seahorses flee before you."

"We are the greatest horses of the air," called one. "Come with us and feel our strength."

Toby felt himself lifted and carried on a fierce wild wind. Paul clung fast to him, shouting with excitement. They were galloping side by side with the rushing herd. Higher and higher the wind horses surged until suddenly they fell away and Toby and his rider floated alone among the stars.

Past the Dog Star they flew, past the Great Bear and the Little Bear, past Cygnus the Swan. Then, right in their path, reared a blazing glory—a huge horse with a shapely head and a brilliant eye, a horse of shining silver that dazzled their eyes.

"Welcome, Toby!" The voice seemed all around them like the air itself. "I am the one you seek. I am Pegasus, the Horse Star, the greatest of all."

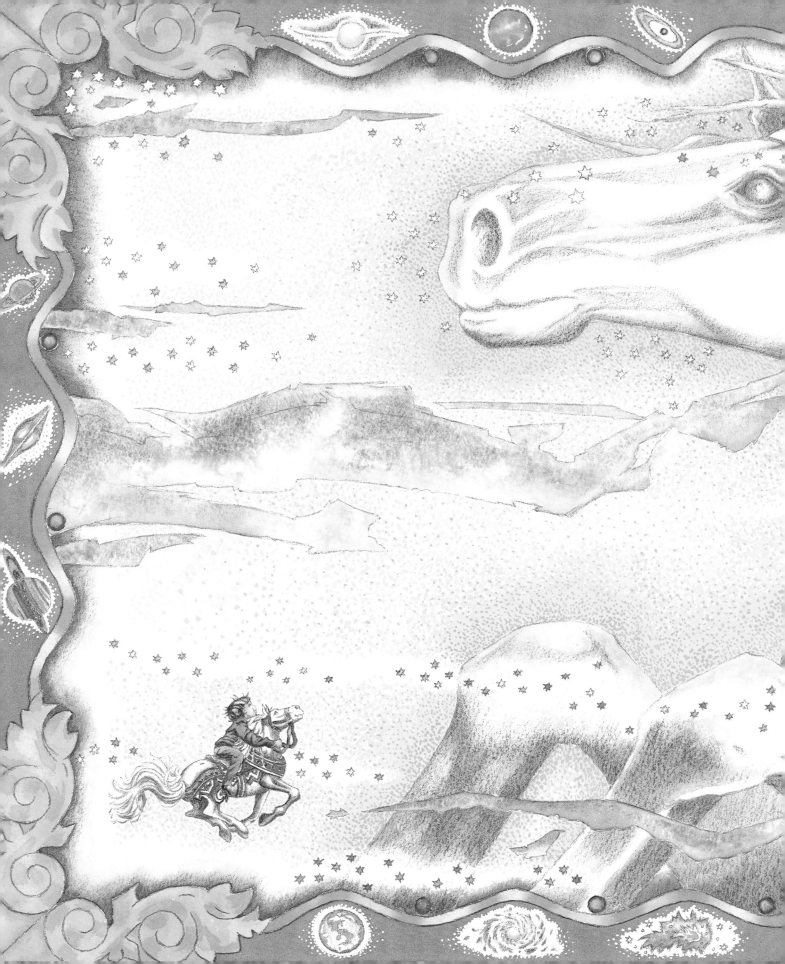

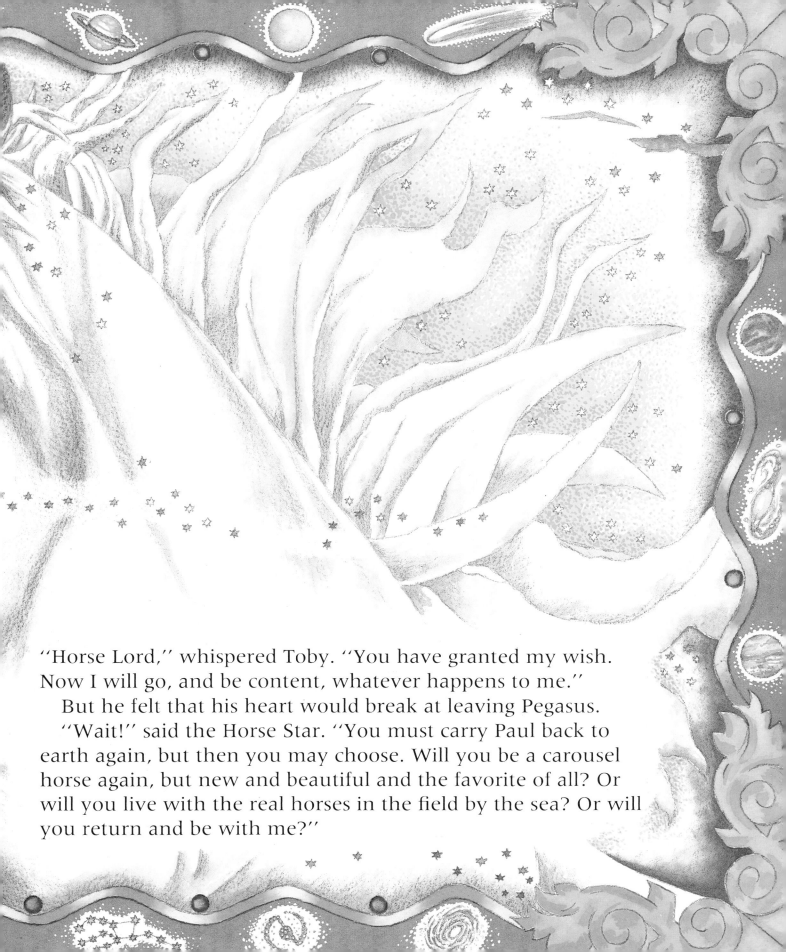

"Horse Lord," whispered Toby. "You have granted my wish. Now I will go, and be content, whatever happens to me."

But he felt that his heart would break at leaving Pegasus.

"Wait!" said the Horse Star. "You must carry Paul back to earth again, but then you may choose. Will you be a carousel horse again, but new and beautiful and the favorite of all? Or will you live with the real horses in the field by the sea? Or will you return and be with me?"

Toby gazed longingly at the Horse Star. Then he turned his head to nuzzle Paul's hand.

"Great One, I cannot leave my friend. I must go back with him."

"No," said Paul. "After this I'd never be happy if you were just a carousel horse again."

Pegasus bent his lordly head until his warm breath touched them. They felt themselves drifting through darkness and stars, down and down till they stood on solid earth close to the fairground. Paul slid down and kissed Toby on the nose.

"Goodbye, Toby. Be happy."

The soft muzzle rubbed his hand and then Paul found himself alone. Above his head a small bright star flashed upward, trailing fire like a meteor, and he laughed to see it go.

The next morning the carousel owner was puzzled not to find Toby in his usual place. But every night Paul looked at the sky before he went to sleep. He knew that, far overhead, a star too tiny for any astronomer to see would be glittering joyfully at the feet of Pegasus.